Harder To
Breathe

By: Britt Wolfe

This Novella Is Dedicated to:

Everyone is America who lives in fear, for everyone standing against hate, bigotry, and ignorance – this is for you.

To those who love boldly, who fight fiercely, who refuse to be silenced – you are seen. You are valued. You are loved. Your courage lights the path forward in a world that so often tries to pull us back.

This is for every stolen moment. Every quiet act of defiance, and every heart that beats for justice. Your existence is resistance, and your hope is powerful. Never forget: you belong here, just as you are.

Harder To Breathe
Is Inspired by: *Down Bad*
by Taylor Swift

Since the release of The Tortured Poets Department, Taylor Swift's *Down Bad* has always stood out to me as a story about a love so all-encompassing it feels like a different world—like an alien abduction. It's the kind of love that feels too extraordinary, too profound, to exist in our harsh reality. But in her lyrics, there's also this eerie undercurrent: a reminder of the ways the world's cruelty can infiltrate even the purest love, of how the pressures and fears we can't escape make that otherworldly connection feel fleeting and vulnerable.

In today's world, where personal choices like who we love are made political and immigration continues to be a lightning rod for fear and hate, I wanted to take that ethereal, almost surreal love story and ground it in a reality that feels foreign in its harshness but all too real for so many. This story, inspired by Swift's extraordinary lyrics, is my effort to bring those emotions into a world where love itself is a risk—a world where the boundaries drawn by privilege, borders, and politics threaten to unravel even the most sacred of bonds.

Yet, even within this tension, this is a story of love—of two boys who found something rare and beautiful in a world that wanted to tear them apart. It's about the strength and bravery of stolen moments, of daring to love even when the world tells you not to. But it's also about the weight of reality, about the forces that feel too great to fight, and the painful truth that sometimes love isn't enough to change the world around you. Even so, it leaves a mark—an unshakable proof that it was real, that it mattered, and I hope this story resonates with you as deeply as Taylor's music always has with me—an ode to the beauty of connection, the power of love, and the defiance of choosing hope in the face of impossibility.

Peace, Love, and Inspiration,

Britt Wolfe

Even The Sun Holds Its Breath For Us

The Texas sun blazed high overhead, drenching the sprawling ranch in a golden haze. The air shimmered faintly in the distance, heat waves rising off the dry, cracked earth and blending with the endless horizon. It was the kind of summer day that seemed to stretch on forever, heavy with the perfume of wildflowers and sun-baked grass. A lone hawk circled lazily in the cobalt sky, its cry echoing faintly across the open fields.

Noah lay on his back in the middle of the hill, his shirt discarded nearby, the warmth of the earth beneath him seeping into his skin. His chest rose and fell in a languid rhythm, his breathing slow, as if the heat had pressed pause on time itself. A faint sheen of sweat glistened on his chest and arms, catching the sunlight as he lazily draped one arm behind his head. Matteo lay beside him, his dark curls tumbling across his forehead, damp and curling tighter in the humidity of his own sweat. His shirt joined Noah's in the grass, leaving his bronzed skin exposed, muscles catching the golden light with every subtle movement.

The air was alive with the quiet hum of life—the ceaseless buzz of cicadas, the soft rustle of grass swaying gently in the breeze, the occasional call of a meadowlark hidden somewhere in the distance. The land stretched out around them in every direction, an endless sea of yellowed prairie grass dotted with wildflowers—bluebonnets, Indian paintbrushes, and patches of vibrant sunflowers that swayed like a lazy congregation under the sun's gaze.

Matteo's hand rested lightly against Noah's arm, their skin touching in a way that felt so natural, as though they had been sculpted by God Himself to fit together. Matteo's thumb traced small, absent-minded circles along the ridge of Noah's bicep, the soft touch tying them together in their golden afterglow. A light breeze stirred the air, carrying with it the faint smell of cattle from a far-off pasture and the earthy sweetness of mesquite trees dotting the landscape.

Noah turned his head toward Matteo, a slow smile spreading across his face as he took in the sight of him—the lines of his jaw, the faint shadow of stubble catching the light, the dark lashes that framed eyes that had always seemed deeper than the Rio Grande. Matteo's head was tilted back slightly, his gaze fixed on the endless sky above them, his expression content in a way that made Noah's chest swell with something too big to name.

"I could stay here forever," Noah murmured, his voice low and lazy.

Matteo turned his head slightly, his lips quirking into a soft smile that didn't quite reach his eyes. "Forever's a long time," he said, but his tone was light, teasing, the weight of the words slipping away into the hot breeze.

Noah reached out, trailing his fingers along Matteo's jaw before brushing a stray curl from his forehead. "Not long enough," he replied, his voice barely more than a whisper, the words carried away by the cicadas' chorus. Matteo leaned into the touch, his eyes closing for a brief moment so he could soak in the gesture along with the beating sunlight.

The sky above them was impossibly vast, the kind of Texas sky that seemed to stretch on forever, its blue so vibrant it felt almost unreal. Puffy white clouds drifted lazily across it, their edges glowing like they'd been touched by fire. The sun sat high and heavy, bathing the world in a light so bright it made the colours seem sharper—the gold of the grass, the deep green of the mesquites, the reds and purples of the wildflowers that dotted the hill like scattered jewels.

Matteo rolled onto his side, propping himself up on one elbow as he looked down at Noah. The sunlight painted him in shades of honey and bronze, and the look in his eyes was so soft, so unguarded, that it made Noah's throat tighten. Matteo reached out, running his fingers lightly over Noah's chest, tracing the faint lines of his collarbone, his touch slow and reverent.

"You look like you belong here," Matteo said, his voice warm and thick, like molasses dripping from a jar. "Like you're part of the land."

Noah let out a soft laugh, shaking his head as he gazed up at Matteo. "Says the guy who looks like he was carved out of sunlight."

Matteo smiled, ducking his head for a moment, a faint blush creeping up his neck. The sight of it made Noah's chest ache in the best way, and he reached up, his hand cupping Matteo's cheek, his thumb brushing lightly across his skin.

The moment stretched between them, quiet and endless, the world around them fading into a blur of gold and green. For now, there was no tomorrow, no family expectations, no weight of the world pressing down on their shoulders. There was only this—this hill, this heat, this love that felt as endless as the Texas summer.

Matteo lay back again, stretching his arms above his head as the prairie grass tickled his skin. He let out a sigh, long and content, his lips quirking into a contented smile as he watched the clouds drift by.

"I bet you didn't know Texan clouds could be this lazy," he said, his voice soft, teasing, like the breeze that carried his words.

Noah turned onto his side to face him, propping his head on his hand as his other hand trailed idly through the warm grass between them. "Everything is lazy in this heat," he said, his grin tilting lopsided. "Even the cows are too hot to move."

Matteo laughed, a quiet sound that rumbled low in his chest, but it faded quickly. His gaze wandered to the horizon, where the land blurred into a shimmering haze of heat and sky. "I think I'd like to be a cloud," he said after a moment, his voice quieter now. "Just... floating. No expectations. No place I'm supposed to be."

Noah frowned slightly, his fingers brushing against Matteo's. "You don't like where you are?"

Matteo turned his head to look at him, the sun casting long shadows across his face, his expression suddenly harder to read. "I like being here," he said, his eyes holding Noah's for a moment too long. "With you. It's the only place that feels real."

Noah swallowed, the warmth of Matteo's words mingling with a chill he couldn't quite shake. "So what's wrong?" he asked, his voice soft, cautious.

Matteo didn't answer right away. He pulled a strand of grass from the ground, twirling it between his fingers as if it could hold the weight of the words he couldn't yet say, and the worries that gripped his chest. "Sometimes I feel like we're just playing a game," he said finally, his voice barely more than a murmur. "Like we're pretending this can go on forever."

Noah's stomach tightened. He reached for Matteo's hand, stilling the restless motion of his fingers. "It doesn't have to be pretend," he said, his voice steadier than he felt. "We've made it work this long," Noah said, reflecting on the previous two years of their relationship.

Matteo's gaze fell to their joined hands, his thumb brushing absently over Noah's knuckles. "Yeah," he said, his tone hollow. "But how much longer before somebody finds out? Before somebody says something?"

Noah's jaw clenched, and for a moment, he didn't trust himself to speak. He hated the fear in Matteo's voice, hated the way their worlds forced it on them. "They won't," he said firmly, though the words felt more like a plea than a promise. "We're careful. Nobody knows."

Matteo gave him a faint, sad smile, one that made Noah's chest ache. "You really believe that? Out here, in the middle of all this—" he gestured at the land around them, vast and golden and quiet "—it feels like we're the only people in the world. But back there—" his voice faltered, his eyes flicking toward the distant silhouette of the ranch house, white and gleaming against the sky. "Back there, it's different."

Noah's gaze followed Matteo's, the sight of his family's grand house suddenly heavier, sharper. "Nobody knows," he said again, his voice quieter this time. "And even if they did... I'd fight for us. You know that, right?"

Matteo didn't answer right away. He sat up, resting his elbows on his knees as his gaze wandered back to the horizon. The sunlight caught the gold in his eyes, but there was a shadow there, too, one that Noah couldn't ignore.

"It's not just us, Noah," Matteo said finally, his voice low, carrying the weight of something that had been building for far too long. "It's your family. If they knew... if they even suspected... you know what they'd do. To me. To my family."

Noah frowned, his stomach twisting as he sat up beside Matteo. The sun beat down on his bare shoulders, but it wasn't the heat making his skin prickle now. "They don't have to know," he said firmly, his voice tight. "We're careful. No one's going to find out," he repeated.

Matteo let out a short, bitter laugh, his eyes fixed on the horizon. "You think they don't already know something's going on? You think your dad hasn't noticed the way you always find excuses to come out here? The way you're always looking at me when you think no one else is watching?"

Noah opened his mouth to protest, but Matteo shook his head, cutting him off. "You've got to understand, Noah—your family wouldn't just disapprove. They'd destroy us. Do you think your father would let me and my family keep working here if he found out? Do you think he'd let me and my family even stay in this country? No way. We'd be right back to Mexico."

The words hit Noah like a slap, and he looked away, his jaw tightening. Matteo's voice softened, but the pain in it only deepened. "And it's not just your family," he said quietly. "My parents... they'd never understand this. They'd never forgive me. I don't think they'd forgive you, either."

Noah's hand moved to Matteo's back, his palm pressing against the damp, sun-warmed skin there. He could feel Matteo's tension, the unsteady rise and fall of his breaths, and it made his chest ache. "I don't care what they think," Noah said, his voice low and fierce. "They don't get to decide this. They don't get to tell us how to feel, or who to love."

Matteo turned to him then, his eyes dark and searching, ooking for something he wasn't sure he'd find. "That's easy for you to say," he murmured. "You'll still have a home, no matter what happens. Your family might hate me, but they'll never throw you out. They'll never send you away."

Noah's chest tightened, the truth of Matteo's words settling over him like a heavy weight he didn't want to acknowledge. He hated it—hated the divide that stood between them, the invisible line drawn by power and privilege, by borders and birthrights. "It's not fair," he said softly, his voice cracking. "None of this is fair."

"No, it's not," Matteo said simply, his gaze drifting back to the sky. "But that doesn't change what it is."

Noah stared at him, his hand still resting on Matteo's back, as the words he wanted to say tangled in his throat. He wanted to tell Matteo that they'd find a way—that their love was stronger than the hate pressing down on them from all sides and in so many different ways. But laying on this hill, surrounded by the vast, sun-drenched expanse of the ranch, he couldn't help but feel the weight of everything that lay beyond it.

"I won't let them hurt you," Noah said finally. "I swear to God, Matteo, I'll do whatever it takes to keep you safe."

Matteo smiled faintly, but it still didn't reach his eyes. "You can't protect me from all of this," he said, his tone gentle. "Not from your father. Not from the law. Not from everything that comes with being who I am and who we are together. But you... you could lose everything, Noah. And I couldn't live with that."

Noah shook his head, his grip tightening on Matteo. "You're everything to me. If I lose them, fine. If I lose all of it, I don't care. None of it matters without you."

Matteo's eyes softened, and he reached up, his hand brushing lightly over Noah's cheek. "You say that now," he said quietly. "But love doesn't fix everything, Noah. It doesn't make the world stop being cruel." Growing up in Mexico and then entering Texas illegally in the dead of night, Matteo knew a little bit more about the cruelty of the world than Noah.

For a long moment, they just sat there, the weight of the conversation settling over them like the heat of the sun. The cicadas hummed their relentless tune, and the wind stirred the grass around them, but the world felt quieter somehow, as if it were holding its breath knowing what lay ahead for these star-crossed lovers.

Finally, Noah leaned forward, pressing his forehead against Matteo's. "I don't care about any of it," he whispered, his voice barely audible. "All I care about is you."

Matteo closed his eyes, his breath catching, and for a moment, the tension of their situation melted away, leaving only the warmth of their skin, the rhythm of their hearts, and the unspoken hope that maybe, just maybe, they could hold on to this, hold onto each other, a little longer.

The golden light of late afternoon wrapped around them like a blanket and it felt like the whole of Texas fell into a gentle lull, just for them. Matteo's head rested against Noah's chest, his arm draped lazily over his waist. The heat of the day had settled into a pleasant warmth, and a breeze stirred the prairie grass around them, carrying with it the faint, earthy scent of the ranch's sunbaked soil. Noah ran his fingers absently through Matteo's dark curls, his touch slow and deliberate, as though trying to commit every strand to memory.

Matteo tilted his face up, his gaze meeting Noah's, and for a moment, neither of them spoke. The only sound was the hum of the cicadas and the soft rustle of the grass as the breeze rolled through it. Noah's fingers paused, and his hand cupped Matteo's cheek, his thumb brushing against the rigid line of his jaw. Matteo leaned into the touch, his eyes fluttering closed, and when Noah kissed him, it was as soft and unhurried as the Texas afternoon, a moment suspended in time.

It was the kind of kiss that carried more than words could hold—a mingling of devotion, longing, and the fear that every moment like this might be their last. Matteo's hand slid to the nape of Noah's neck, pulling him closer, and the kiss deepened, their breath mingling as the sun dipped lower in the sky. When they finally broke apart, their foreheads rested together, and Noah couldn't help but smile at the faint curve of Matteo's lips, the way his cheeks flushed a soft, earthy beige as the sun began to sink lower in the sky.

"Stay here with me forever," Noah whispered, his voice thick with emotion.

Matteo laughed softly, a sound that was warm and rich and entirely his. "Forever doesn't fit in a day," he murmured, but his arm tightened around Noah's waist, and for a while, they simply lay there, letting the sun sink lower into the horizon.

Sleep claimed them gently, their bodies pressed close as the heat of the day gave way to the coolness of evening. When Matteo woke, it was to the sound of distant voices—sharp, urgent, cutting through the stillness like the crack of a whip. His heart leapt into his throat as he sat up, his gaze snapping to the hill's crest, where the faint silhouette of men appeared against the amber sky.

"Noah," Matteo hissed, shaking his shoulder. "Noah, wake up."

Noah stirred, blinking groggily as the shouting grew louder, the words still too far off to make out but the tone unmistakable. He sat up quickly, his heart pounding as he followed Matteo's gaze. The workers—his family's workers—were coming. Among them, he could make out the broad, familiar frame of Matteo's father, his voice carrying over the hill.

"Shit," Noah muttered, scrambling to his feet. He snatched Matteo's shirt from the ground and thrust it toward him. "Go. Now."

"Noah—" Matteo started, but Noah cut him off, his tone sharp, panicked.

"Go! They can't see you here!"

Matteo hesitated for a moment, his gaze flicking to Noah's, but the urgency in his voice left no room for argument. He took the shirt and pulled it over his head in one swift motion, then glanced back at Noah, his jaw tight with worry.

"Be careful," he whispered, his voice barely audible over the distant voices.

Noah nodded, his throat tight, and Matteo turned, disappearing into the tall grass as the last rays of sunlight painted the world in gold and shadow. Noah watched him go, his chest aching, before turning back toward the approaching group. He grabbed his own shirt, hastily pulling it on as he started walking toward them, forcing himself to steady his breathing and push down the knot of fear twisting in his stomach.

The men reached him just as the sun dipped below the horizon, the first hints of twilight casting long shadows across the land. Their faces were shadowed, but the suspicion in their voices was clear.

"There you are," one of the men said, his voice rough and edged with annoyance. "We've been looking for you."

Noah shrugged, forcing a casualness he didn't feel. "I was out here checking the fencing," he said smoothly, gesturing vaguely toward the hill behind him. "Didn't realize it was so late."

Matteo's father, Héctor, stepped forward then, his expression hard, his eyes sharp as they fixed on Noah. "You see my boy out here?" he asked, his voice low and direct. "Matteo. He was supposed to meet me an hour ago, but he never showed."

Noah's stomach clenched, but he didn't let it show. Instead, he shook his head, his tone cool, measured. "Haven't seen him," he lied, the words coming easily, too easily. "I've been out here alone."

Matteo's father narrowed his eyes, studying him for a moment longer, and Noah forced himself to hold his gaze, to look calm, unbothered. "You're sure?" the man pressed.

"Yeah," Noah said firmly, his voice steady. "If I see him, I'll send him your way."

There was a beat of silence, the weight of the moment pressing down on Noah like the fading heat of the day, before Matteo's father gave a curt nod. "You do that," he said gruffly, turning to follow the other workers as they began to fan out across the field.

Noah stood there, his hands clenched into fists at his sides, watching them disappear into the twilight. His heart was pounding, his chest tight, but he forced himself to stand tall, to keep the mask of indifference firmly in place. He didn't move until the last of the voices had faded, the workers' shouts swallowed by the night.

Only then did he exhale, the lie he had told settling over him like a stone. He turned back toward the hill, the spot where Matteo had disappeared, and his chest ached with the knowledge of what he had just done—and what he hadn't.

Because no matter how much he loved Matteo, no matter how much he wanted to fight for them, he wasn't ready. Not yet. Not when the world around them would tear them apart the moment it knew the truth.

The Weight Of Hate

The bunkhouse smelled of sweat and coffee, the thick scent of last night's rain still clinging to the air despite the dry heat rolling in through the open door. It was barely past five, the sky outside painted in inky blues and purples, the first hints of dawn bleeding through the horizon. The ranch was already stirring—boots scuffing against the packed dirt, the distant clang of metal as someone checked the fencing, the low murmur of voices as men shuffled through their morning routines.

Noah sat at the worn wooden table near the back of the room, hunched over a steaming mug, the soft glow of the television casting flickering shadows against the walls. Matteo sat across from him, pretending not to notice the way Noah's knee bounced beneath the table, pretending not to know the exact cadence of his breath. This morning, they were just two ranch hands, well technically, Noah was the rancher's son, but they were just two young men sharing space before the day started. That was the story they told the world. That was the story they had to tell themselves in these moments where eyes could see them.

The TV crackled, the voice of a news anchor cutting through the low hum of conversation.

"This morning, federal agents have begun mass deportations across southern Texas, enforcing the new executive order signed by President Langford last month. The administration has vowed to crack down on illegal crossings, workplace violations, and long-term undocumented residents—"

A chair scraped against the floor as one of the ranch hands, a broad man with a thick drawl, Rusty Carter, let out a low whistle. "'Bout damn time," he muttered, stretching his arms above his head. "Shoulda happened years ago. Gettin' real tired of payin' taxes so these illegals can live off our hard work."

Matteo felt his stomach drop, the words slamming into him like a fist to the ribs. He clenched his jaw, forcing his face into something unreadable. He'd spent his whole life perfecting that look—calm, unaffected, just another worker who knew better than to speak up. But inside, his pulse roared like floodwaters breaking free from a dam.

Beside him, Noah shifted in his seat. Matteo didn't look at him. He didn't have to. He knew what was coming.

"That's the truth," Noah said, his voice steady, easy. "They come here, take what isn't theirs, send the money back home. Hell, half of 'em don't even speak English."

Matteo felt his throat tighten, bile rising. He told himself that Noah was just playing a role, trying to blend in, but the words stung. This was a far cry from the day before on the hill when Noah said he would fight for them and for their love.

Rusty chuckled, taking a swig of his coffee. "Damn right. They oughta line 'em up and march 'em right back across the border."

Noah let out a sharp laugh, shaking his head. "Hell, we wouldn't even need mass deportations if people just quit givin' these parasites a reason to stay. No jobs, no housing, no handouts—send 'em back to whatever shithole they crawled out of. Watch how fast they scurry across the border when they realize this country isn't theirs to leech off anymore."

Matteo kept his eyes on his hands, fingers curled around his chipped ceramic mug, his knuckles tight. He didn't move, didn't flinch. But inside, something cracked.

The conversation shifted—someone complaining about the heat, another man joking about how many rattlesnakes they'd see today—but the weight of Noah's words sat heavy in Matteo's chest, pressing against his ribs like a slow, suffocating hand.

He wanted to be surprised. He wanted to believe Noah had choked on the words, that they had burned coming out. But Matteo knew better.

Noah had said what he'd said because he had to. Because this world belonged to men like Rusty, men who didn't think twice about the damage they inflicted with their careless cruelty. Because in this place, among these people, Noah could never be anything other than one of them.

And Matteo—Matteo was something to be erased.

Outside, the land stretched out in endless waves of gold and dust, the rising sun washing the world in pale amber light. More ranch hands were moving about, rounding up the cattle, securing the fences, preparing for another brutal summer day. Matteo and his father, Héctor worked together, Matteo's body on autopilot, his hands gripping the worn leather reins of his horse as he and Héctor rode toward the northern fields.

Héctor rode slightly ahead, his broad back rigid, his shoulders set like stone. He had said nothing when the news played that morning, had not even acknowledged the conversation that followed. But Matteo had seen the tension in his jaw, the flicker of something dark in his gaze.

His father had been in this country for almost as long as Matteo had been alive. He had built his life on this land, had broken his body for wages that barely kept food on their table. He had brought Matteo here, raised him here, taught him how to ride almost before he could walk, taught him the dignity of hard work.

And now, with a single executive order, it could all be torn away.

President Langford had built his campaign on hate. He had promised to take back America, to make it "pure" again. And the people had cheered—not because they believed he could fix their lives, not because they thought he would make anything better. They had voted for him because he would hurt the people they hated. Because they wanted to watch families like Matteo's be ripped apart.

Matteo swallowed hard, his grip tightening on the reins.

The thing about growing up undocumented was that you learned to live with uncertainty. You carried it in your bones, in the spaces between your ribs. Every day, every hour, there was the knowledge that everything you loved, everything you had built, could disappear in an instant.

But this—this was something different. This was the beginning of the end.

And Noah—Noah had chosen his side, not that he had much of a choice. Even if Noah chose him, there was no protecting Matteo from what was coming.

Matteo had known this was coming. He had told himself it didn't matter, that he could live with Noah's silence, with the distance they had to maintain in public. But hearing Noah's voice, hearing those words spill so effortlessly from his mouth—it was different.

It was a wound, fresh and raw, that no amount of love could stitch back together.

The morning sun was relentless, casting a shimmering haze over the sprawling fields. The horses' hooves kicked up dust as Matteo and Héctor rode, their shadows trailing long and lean across the cracked earth. Matteo adjusted his hat against the glare, his gaze fixed on the horizon, where the distant line of mesquite trees stood like sentinels guarding the edge of the world.

They had been riding in silence for some time, the quiet filled only with the rhythmic creak of saddle leather and the soft snorts of their horses. Matteo felt the tension radiating from his father, saw it in the way Héctor's broad shoulders were squared and his hands gripped the reins just a little too tightly. He knew what was coming—had felt it building ever since morning coffee in the bunkhouse—but still, he wasn't ready when Héctor finally spoke.

"We need to talk," Héctor said, once they had put enough distance between themselves and the other ranch hands. He didn't look at Matteo, his gaze fixed straight ahead as if the words were easier to say without meeting his son's eyes.

Matteo's chest tightened, and he glanced at his father out of the corner of his eye. "What about?" he asked, though he already knew the answer.

Héctor let out a slow breath, shifting in the saddle. "This place isn't safe for us anymore," he said. "We can't stay here."

The words hit Matteo like a blow, even though he'd been bracing for them. He tightened his grip on the reins, his knuckles whitening. "We've been here almost my whole life," he said quietly, his voice tight with emotion. "We've worked this land. It's... it's our home."

Héctor finally turned to look at him, his dark eyes heavy with the weight of what he was about to say. "It was never ours, mijo," he said softly. "You know that. This land belongs to them—always has. And now, with everything happening, they're going to make sure we know it. Maybe not the Calloways themselves, but people like them."

Matteo swallowed hard, his throat dry as the desert wind. He looked away, his gaze sweeping over the fields that had been his whole world for so long. The thought of leaving was unbearable, but deep down, he knew his father was right. He'd known it since the recent election. The tides of America were turning toward hatred, bigotry and intolerance. There was blame only for the different ones, not for the billionaires who profited off the millions of Americans doing it rough and eking out a life.

"They're going to come here, Matteo," Héctor continued, his voice growing firmer. "Maybe not today, maybe not tomorrow, but they will. And when they do, it won't just be us who pay the price."

Matteo's head snapped toward him, confusion and fear flickering in his eyes. "What do you mean?"

Héctor's jaw tightened, his gaze darkening. "If this ranch gets raided, they won't just take us. They'll tear this place apart. They'll look at everyone here—every man who speaks Spanish, every family that looks like ours—and they'll drag them all down with us. And The Calloways..." His voice softened at the mention of Noah's family, the owner's of the land they worked, but the words hit Matteo harder than any shout could have. "The Calloways have been good to us and they could get caught up in this too."

Matteo's stomach twisted painfully. "Noah's family is rich. Surely their money will keep them safe," he said, though his voice wavered with doubt.

"Maybe," Héctor said, his tone sharp. "But money won't mean a damn thing if they find out they've been trying to protect us. They'll call it aiding and abetting. They'll make an example out of them."

Matteo's chest ached, and he gripped the reins tighter, his horse shifting restlessly beneath him. His father spoke of the Calloway family, but Matteo thought only of Noah. The thought of Noah being hurt, being dragged into this nightmare, was unbearable. Despite everything Noah had said that morning and all the mornings before, Matteo wanted to believe he was only trying to survive in a world that wouldn't let them be honest. And despite the sting of those words, Matteo loved Noah. Loved him enough to leave, if it meant keeping him safe.

"What are we supposed to do?" Matteo asked, his voice breaking slightly. "Just pack up and disappear?"

"Yes," Héctor said simply, his tone leaving no room for argument. "We pack what we can carry and we go. Tonight."

Matteo shook his head, his mind racing. "Where will we go? How will we—"

"We'll figure it out," Héctor interrupted, his voice firm. "We've done it before, and we'll do it again. But staying here isn't an option anymore."

Matteo fell silent, his chest heaving as he tried to process what his father was saying. Their horses plodded on, their hooves striking a steady rhythm against the ground, but Matteo felt like the world was crumbling beneath him.

"I don't want anyone to get hurt," Matteo said after a long pause, his voice barely above a whisper. "Noah...I mean, the Calloways don't deserve that." He said without thinking what the words might mean to his dad.

Héctor glanced at him, his expression softening for a moment. "I know, mijo," he said gently. "That's why we're leaving. To protect ourselves. To do what is right by people who have done what is right by us for so many years."

Matteo nodded slowly, though the weight of leaving Noah felt crushing especially as he was unable to share the pain of it with anyone else. Matteo looked out at the horizon, where the sun was still rising higher and higher, bathing the fields in hues of amber and gold. He thought of Noah's face, the way he smiled when he thought no one was looking, the way his voice softened when they were alone. The thought of never seeing him again felt like a knife twisting in his chest.

But Héctor was right. They couldn't stay. Not if they wanted to survive. Not if Matteo wanted to keep Noah safe.

"Okay," Matteo said finally, his voice trembling. "We'll go."

Héctor nodded, his shoulders relaxing slightly. "I spoked with your mother this morning," he said. "She and your sister are making preparations. We'll leave tonight after it gets dark."

Matteo didn't respond. He just kept his eyes on the horizon, trying to memorize every detail of the land he was about to leave behind. He told himself it was for the best—that this was the only way. But no matter how hard he tried, he couldn't stop the tears that burned at the edges of his eyes, or the ache in his chest that told him he was leaving more than just a home behind.

He knew he had to leave, but he wouldn't leave without saying goodbye to Noah.

The Heat Of Goodbye

The late afternoon sun was merciless, hanging low in the sky, gilding the fields with a harsh, hot golden light. Dust clung to the air, stirred by every movement, shimmering in the oppressive heat. Matteo worked beside Héctor, their shoulders brushing occasionally as they moved through the field. His father's presence was a steadying force, but Matteo's mind was elsewhere—adrift in the weight of what the evening would bring.

Noah's voice broke through the rhythmic clink of tools and the soft shuffling of their boots on the dry earth. "Matteo," he called, his tone casual, almost too much so. Matteo stiffened, not daring to meet his father's gaze in case there was suspicion in them.

Noah strode toward them, his shirt sleeves rolled to his elbows, a thin sheen of sweat glistening on his tanned skin. His grin was easy, though Matteo could see the tightness at the corners of his mouth. "I need Matteo for something," he said, not waiting for or needing permission as he gestured for Matteo to follow. Héctor glanced between the two, his brow furrowing slightly, but he said nothing.

Matteo hesitated, his heart pounding. The events of the morning still lingered between them. But he nodded, stepping away from his father without a word. Noah's hand brushed against Matteo's back briefly as they walked, a fleeting touch hidden by the angle of their movement. It burned like a brand.

They moved in silence, the air between them taut as a wire. Noah led Matteo toward the old barn—a weathered structure standing stubbornly against time, its wood faded and cracked from years of sun and storms. Matteo's breath caught as they approached, memories flooding him with each step. This place had been their haven once, the site of stolen kisses and whispered promises when they were still too young to fully understand the enormity of them.

Noah pushed the barn door open with a creak, the dim interior cool and quiet, a stark contrast to the relentless sun outside. The scent of hay and aged wood wrapped around them, familiar and comforting. Matteo's footsteps faltered as Noah turned to face him, his blue eyes burning with raw passion.

"Come here," Noah said, his voice low, urgent. Before Matteo could respond, Noah was pulling him close, his hands gripping Matteo's arms as their bodies pressed together. Matteo let out a shaky breath, his resolve crumbling as Noah's lips found his.

The kiss was desperate, hungry, as if Noah were trying to pour everything he couldn't say into it. Matteo's hands gripped Noah's shoulders instinctively, but his mind was elsewhere, racing with thoughts of his father's words, of the bags already packed, of the horizon that would soon carry him away.

Noah pulled back, his brow furrowing as he searched Matteo's face. "What's wrong?" he asked, his voice soft with worry.

Matteo shook his head, trying to pull away, but Noah held him fast. "Nothing," he muttered, but the words felt hollow, even to him.

Noah's grip tightened, his voice rising slightly. "Don't lie to me, Matteo. I know you. Tell me what's going on."

Matteo swallowed hard, his chest tightening as the truth clawed its way to the surface. "We're leaving," he said finally, his voice barely more than a whisper. "Tonight."

Noah's hands fell away as he took a step back, his eyes narrowing. "What?" he asked, his voice sharp with disbelief.

Matteo forced himself to meet Noah's gaze, his heart breaking at the hurt he saw there. "My dad... he says it's not safe here anymore. We have to go."

"No," Noah said firmly, shaking his head as if the sheer force of his denial could change reality. "You're not leaving. You can't."

"We don't have a choice," Matteo said, his voice trembling. "If we stay—if they find us—it won't just be my family that gets hurt. It'll be yours too. You. And I can't let that happen."

Noah stepped forward, his hands gripping Matteo's shoulders again, harder this time. "I don't care about that," he said fiercely. "I don't care about any of it. You're not leaving me, Matteo."

Matteo's chest ached, but he forced himself to stay firm, to pull away from Noah's grasp. "This is the only way," he said, his voice breaking. "I have to protect you."

"Protect me?" Noah's voice rose, anger flashing in his eyes. "You think running away is protecting me? You think leaving me here, alone, is the answer? This is what, supposed to be romantic? Leaving me safe...and just stranded?"

"Noah—" Matteo started, but the words caught in his throat as Noah shoved him back, his movements abrupt, violent in their frustration.

"You're a coward," Noah spat, his voice laced with venom. "You'd rather run, leave me in your dust, than fight for us. And you know what? Maybe I was wrong about you."

Matteo flinched, his heart shattering under the weight of Noah's words. He stepped forward, his hands reaching for Noah's, but Noah pulled away, his eyes blazing with anger. "Noah, please," Matteo said desperately. "I'm doing this for you. For us."

Noah laughed bitterly, the sound sharp and cruel. "For us?" he repeated, his voice dripping with disdain. "You're running because you're scared. Don't pretend this is about me."

Matteo opened his mouth to argue, but Noah was already turning away, his hands clenched into fists at his sides. As he reached the barn door, he threw one final look over his shoulder, his expression hard.

"Fuck it," he said coldly. "If I can't have us, then what's the point?"

The door slammed behind him, the sound echoing through the barn like a gunshot. Matteo stood there, his chest heaving, the silence that followed heavier than any words. The walls seemed to close in around him, the weight of Noah's anger pressing down until it was even harder to breathe.

The sun dipped lower in the sky as Matteo stood alone in the barn, his breathing shallow and uneven. The air felt heavier, weighed down by the echoes of Noah's anger, the slam of the door still reverberating through his chest. Dust motes danced in the beams of golden light filtering through the cracks in the wooden walls, but the barn felt darker now, emptier. It was a place that had once been theirs—a sanctuary, a secret—but now it felt like it might collapse under what just happened.

Matteo dragged a hand down his face, trying to steady himself. His throat ached with unshed tears, but he swallowed them down, forcing his feet to move. He stepped outside into the late afternoon heat, the glare of the sun momentarily blinding him as he adjusted his hat. The ranch stretched out before him, golden and sprawling, the familiar hum of cicadas and the low moo of cattle drifting through the air.

He had to keep going. He had to. There was no time to linger, no time to fall apart. His father's voice echoed in his mind—steady, resolute: We'll leave tonight. Matteo's heart clenched at the thought, but he couldn't let himself falter. This wasn't just about him. It was about his family. It was about Noah, too, whether Noah saw it that way or not.

He walked back toward the fields where his father was still working, his boots crunching against the dry earth. The heat bore down on him like a physical weight, each step heavier than the last. He spotted Héctor in the distance, his broad shoulders bent as he worked the reins of his horse, guiding it through the dry grass. The sight of him brought a small measure of comfort, even as Matteo's chest tightened with the knowledge of what he was about to leave behind.

When Héctor looked up and saw him approaching, his brow furrowed slightly. Matteo knew his father could see the tension in his face, the heaviness in his steps. Matteo hoped what his father saw in him was chalked up to leaving the land and not about leaving anything, or anyone else. Héctor said nothing. He simply nodded.

The work was familiar, repetitive, almost meditative. Matteo focused on the rhythmic swing of his hammer, the dull thud of steel against wood, the sweat dripping down his back as he worked. He let the motion carry him, let it push the storm of emotions swirling in his chest to the edges of his mind. But no matter how hard he tried, he couldn't shake the image of Noah's face—the anger in his eyes, the venom in his voice, the way he'd said, "If I can't have us, then what's the point?"

The words lingered like a wound that wouldn't stop bleeding.

Héctor worked beside him in silence for a while, the only sounds the creak of the fence and the soft rustle of the prairie grass in the Texas wind. Finally, he spoke, his voice low, as if sensing the storm raging inside his son. "Sometimes," he said, not looking up from his work, "doing the right thing feels like the cruelest thing in the world."

Matteo's hands stilled, the hammer hanging limp in his grip. He stared at the ground, the dry, cracked earth blurred by the haze of tears he refused to let fall.

"It's not fair," Matteo said after a long moment, his voice barely audible. "It's not fair that we've worked so hard, that we've built our lives here, and it can all be taken away just like that. It's not fair that the world is so much bigger than us, but all it does is find ways to make us feel even smaller."

Héctor straightened, wiping the sweat from his brow with the back of his hand. He turned to Matteo, his dark eyes filled with a quiet strength that made Matteo's chest ache. "No, it's not fair," he said simply. "But fairness doesn't pay attention to men like us. Fairness belongs to the ones who make the rules. And we—" he gestured at the land around them, at the horizon painted in amber and gold "—we don't get to make the rules. We just survive them."

Matteo nodded slowly, his grip tightening on the hammer. He wanted to argue, to rail against the injustice of it all, but he knew his father was right.

This was the world they lived in—a world that didn't care about fairness, about love, about the pieces of themselves they had to leave behind.

They worked in silence as the sun began its slow descent, casting long shadows across the fields. Matteo focused on the task in front of him, on the rhythmic swing of the hammer, on the feel of the wood beneath his hands. He tried to lose himself in the work, to push down the ache in his chest, but it was always there, lingering just beneath the surface.

By the time they finished, the sun was a fiery orb sinking into the horizon. Matteo looked out at the land he had called home for so many years, the rolling fields bathed in the warm glow of dusk. He tried to memorize every detail—the way the grass swayed in the breeze, the silhouette of the mesquite trees against the fading light, the distant call of a hawk soaring high above them. He wanted to hold on to it all, to carry it with him, even as he prepared to leave it behind.

Héctor clapped a hand on his shoulder, pulling him from his thoughts. "It's time to head back," he said, his voice betraying his exhaustion.

Matteo nodded, swallowing hard as he followed his father back toward the house. The fear of everything to come settled over him like a heavy blanket, but he kept his head high, his movements steady. This was what he had to do. For his family. For Noah. For himself.

As they reached the edge of the field, Matteo glanced over his shoulder one last time, his gaze lingering on the horizon where the sun had disappeared, leaving behind a sky coloured with the soft, fading lights of twilight. The land stretched out before him, endless and beautiful, a piece of himself woven into every blade of grass, every shadow of the hills. As he turned back toward the house, his heart heavy but resolute, he thought of Noah's words, of the love they had shared, of the impossible choices they had been forced to make. The world was cruel, yes—but it had also given him this, however momentary. And for that, he was grateful.

If I Can't Have Us

Noah stormed out of the barn, his boots kicking up small clouds of dust as he walked across the field. The late afternoon sun was relentless, beating down on him like it wanted to peel away the last of his composure. He kept his gaze fixed on the ground, his jaw clenched tight, his mind a tangle of anger, heartbreak, and disbelief.

He hadn't gone far when his steps faltered, his body pulling him toward the one place he couldn't seem to stay away from—the hill. The hill where he and Matteo had spent so many afternoons tangled together, where the weight of the world seemed to disappear, if only for a while. His breath came fast as he climbed the gentle slope, his chest heaving not from the exertion, but from the storm of hurt and anger raging inside him.

When he reached the top of the hill, he dropped to the ground, his back hitting the warm grass with a force that sent a shock through his body. He stared up at the endless blue sky, the clouds moving lazily overhead, and for a moment, he felt like he was suffocating. His heart pounded in his chest, the rhythm uneven, painful.

Why?

The word echoed in his mind, louder than the cicadas, louder than the distant calling of the cattle. Why was Matteo leaving? Why was this their reality? Why couldn't they have just one thing in this world that didn't feel impossible?

The anger rose in him again, hot and sharp, cutting through the ache in his chest. "Fuck it," he muttered to the sky, his voice trembling. He pressed the heels of his hands against his eyes, as if he could block out the world, as if he could stop himself from seeing Matteo's face, from hearing the tremble in his voice when he said, "This is the only way."

He loved Matteo. God, he loved him so much it felt like it might kill him. But what was love when it couldn't stop the world from tearing them apart? What was love when it left him lying here, alone, on the same hill where they'd once dreamed of forever? Or had Noah been the only one dreaming of forever together?

The memory of Matteo's voice played on a loop in his mind: "This is the only way. I have to protect you." Noah let out a bitter laugh, the sound hollow and sharp. Protect him? Matteo thought this was protection? Leaving Noah behind to face the weight of his absence, to carry the silence that would echo in every corner of this ranch, in every blade of grass on this hill?

"Fuck it," he said again, his voice louder now, rising with the wind. He sat up, his hands gripping the dry earth beneath him. "Fuck it, and fuck him if I can't have us."

The words hung in the air for a moment, raw and heavy. Noah pushed himself to his feet, his legs shaky but resolute. He couldn't just let Matteo leave. Not like this. Not without a fight.

The ranch house was cool and quiet when Noah stepped inside, the heavy wooden door creaking on its hinges. His father, Charles Calloway, was seated at the kitchen table, a cup of coffee in his hand despite the late afternoon hour. He looked up when Noah entered, his brow furrowing at the sight of his son.

"Something wrong?" Charles asked, his voice commanding. Charles, a Christian man, was the leader of this household and his voice carried the gravity of his role, even in casual conversation.

Noah hesitated for only a moment before he walked over to the table, pulling out the chair across from his father. He sat down heavily, his hands resting on the worn surface of the table. "I need to talk to you," he said, his voice tight.

Charles leaned back in his chair, his sharp blue eyes studying Noah. "Go on."

Noah took a deep breath, his hands curling into fists on the table. "Matteo's family is leaving tonight," he said, the words tumbling out before he could stop them. "They're running. They're... they're illegals."

Charles's expression didn't change, but his silence was heavy, pressing down on Noah like the heat of the sun outside. "I obviously know that," Charles said slowly, "so, why are you telling me this?"

Noah looked away, his gaze fixing on the window, where the last light of day cast long shadows across the fields. "Because... because I don't want them to get caught up in something worse," he said, his voice barely more than a whisper. "If they leave here, it's only a matter of time before ICE comes looking. And if they do, it'll be bad for them. And for us."

Charles was quiet for a long moment, his fingers drumming lightly against the side of his mug. When he spoke, his voice was cold, deliberate. "You're saying we should call it in. Report them."

Noah's stomach churned at the words, but he nodded. "It's better this way.

If we report it, they might go easy on us. On you."

Charles's gaze didn't waver. "And you're sure this is the right thing to do?"

Noah hesitated, the weight of the decision pressing down on him like a physical force. He thought of Matteo's face, the way he had looked at him in the barn, the way his voice had trembled when he said goodbye. The memory filled him with a petulant, frustrated rage. "Yes," he said finally, his voice breaking. "It's the only way."

He didn't wait for his father's answer as he headed up the wooden stairs to his bedroom. He sat on his bed, pulling his cell phone from his pocket.

With the call made, Noah laid stretched out on his twin bed, his hands laced behind his head, starring up at the ceiling as the sun sunk below the horizon.

*****

The night was still and oppressive, the air thick with humidity and the faint scent of dust and cattle. Noah stood on the porch of the Calloway ranch house, his hands gripping the wooden railing as he stared out into the darkness. The knowledge of what he'd done sat heavy on his chest, an unbearable pressure that he couldn't shake. Somewhere, deep in the shadows of the ranch, Matteo was preparing to leave. Matteo, who had loved him, trusted him. Matteo, who had no idea what was about to happen.

The sound of engines shattered the stillness first—low, rumbling, and growing louder with every passing second. Noah stiffened, his breath hitching as he turned toward the gravel road leading onto the property.

Headlights cut through the dark, their beams bouncing off the dry grass and the weathered fence posts. One, two, three vehicles—a convoy of white vans and black SUVs, their windows dark, their purpose unmistakable.

ICE – Immigration and Customs Enforcement.

The vehicles rolled to a stop in a cloud of dust, the grinding of tires on gravel sending a shiver down Noah's spine. The doors opened almost simultaneously, and agents spilled out in sharp black uniforms, their movements efficient, purposeful. Their boots hit the ground with a crunch that seemed deafening in the stillness of the night. The ranch that had always felt vast and alive now seemed small, vulnerable, suffocated under the weight of their presence.

One of the agents barked orders, his voice cutting through the dark like the crack of a whip. "You two, secure the perimeter. The rest of you, on me."

Noah's stomach churned as he watched them fan out, flashlights slicing through the night, their beams sweeping over the barn, the fields, the small house that Matteo and his family called home. It was a humble structure, its paint peeling, the porch sagging slightly under the weight of years. It had always been a place of warmth, of laughter and life. Now, it felt like a target.

The lead agent pounded on the front door of the house, his fist heavy and unrelenting. "This is ICE! Open the door! We have a warrant!"

Noah gripped the railing tighter, his knuckles white. The porch creaked under his shifting weight, but he couldn't tear his eyes away. His chest felt like it was caving in, each breath more difficult than the last. This was his doing. These men, this raid, the fear etched into every shadow of the ranch —it was all because of him.

The door opened slowly, creaking on its hinges. Héctor stepped out first, his broad frame filling the doorway, his hands raised in a gesture of surrender. The porch light above him cast harsh shadows across his face, highlighting the deep lines of exhaustion and worry that had only deepened in recent weeks.

"What's this about?" Héctor asked, his voice steady, but Noah could hear the tremor beneath it, the voice of a man who had lived his whole life preparing for this moment and still wasn't ready.

"You're being detained," the lead agent said, his tone clipped and impersonal. "Step outside, hands where we can see them."

Behind Héctor, Matteo's mother appeared, her arms wrapped tightly around their teen-aged daughter, who clung to her mother with wide, tear-filled eyes. Matteo emerged last, his movements slow, deliberate. He stepped in front of his mother and sister, his jaw clenched, his eyes burning with defiance.

Noah's heart twisted painfully at the sight of him. Matteo's dark curls were damp with sweat, his chest rising and falling with quick, shallow breaths. His gaze swept the yard, the barn, the fields, until it landed on the porch where Noah stood frozen. Their eyes met, and for a moment, everything else disappeared—the agents, the shouting, the chaos. It was just them, staring across the gulf that had opened between them, a chasm carved by betrayal.

Noah wanted to look away, but he couldn't. Matteo's expression was unreadable, a mask of calm that couldn't hide the flicker of hurt and disbelief in his eyes. Noah felt like he was drowning, the heaviness of his guilt dragging him under. He wanted to run to Matteo, to pull him close, to tell him that he hadn't meant for it to be like this, he'd just been so angry. But his feet stayed planted, rooted in the porch like they were made of stone.

The agents moved quickly, their voices sharp and commanding as they began cuffing Héctor and Matteo. Matteo didn't resist, his jaw tight, his hands trembling as the cold metal of the handcuffs closed around his wrists. His mother was sobbing quietly.

"Don't fight them," Héctor said quietly, his voice breaking as he glanced back at Matteo. "Just do what they say." The agents began ushering the family to different vans.

Matteo didn't respond, his eyes fixed on Noah as the agents began to lead him toward one of the waiting vans. The distance between them seemed to stretch endlessly, and yet it wasn't enough. Noah could see every detail of Matteo's face—the tears clinging to his lashes, the tension in his jaw, the betrayal etched into every part of him.

As Matteo passed the barn, he stopped suddenly, twisting in the grip of the agents. "Please," he said, his voice breaking. "Let me say goodbye to my family."

The agents hesitated, exchanging a glance, before one of them nodded. Matteo turned back toward his mother and sister, his shoulders shaking as he leaned into them, unable to embrace them properly with his hands cuffed behind his back. His mother whispered something into his ear, her words too soft to hear, but the pain in her voice was unmistakable. Matteo nodded, his face buried in her shoulder, before stepping back and allowing the agents to lead him away.

Noah's throat tightened as Matteo passed him again, his steps heavy, his head held high despite the humiliation and terror of the moment. Matteo didn't look at him this time, his gaze fixed straight ahead as the agents guided him into the back of a van, alone. The door slammed shut with a metallic thud that echoed across the ranch with finality.

The convoy began to pull away, the red taillights disappearing into the night, leaving behind a cloud of dust and a silence that felt deafening. Noah stood on the porch, his chest heaving, his vision blurred with tears he refused to let fall. The ranch felt emptier now, the fields darker, the stars colder.

He had done this. He had called them. He had let them take Matteo and his family. And as he stood there, the weight of that choice settled over him like a suffocating blanket, heavy and unrelenting.

For the first time in his life, Noah understood what it meant to feel truly alone.

The World Was Bigger Than Us

The days after the raid crawled by in slow motion, the summer heat blanketing the ranch. Noah went through the motions of his life, each day bleeding into the next, but the heaviness in his chest never eased even slightly. Guilt clung to him like the dust that settled on the ranch's dry earth, and no matter how hard he tried to shake it off, it followed him. Every hoofbeat, every echo of the cattle's low calls, carried with it the memory of Matteo.

He would see Matteo in the smallest things. In the way the grass waved in the evening breeze, in the faint scent of hay that lingered in the barn. The hill where they had lain together only days before had become a shrine in his mind, to a love he had thrown away. Noah couldn't bring himself to go back there; the sight of the flattened grass where their bodies had pressed together was too much.

And still, Matteo was everywhere. Noah could hear him in the whispers of the wind, feel him in the heat of the Texas sun. Every breath felt like a betrayal, as if the very act of going on without Matteo was proof of his failure and his hasty act of retaliation. Noah had thought the pain might fade, that the sharp edge of his guilt would dull with time. But it didn't. It only grew, gnawing at him until it felt like he might crumble under it.

On the seventh day, he broke.

It happened in the back pasture, where Noah had been running laps under the blazing sun, his shirt soaked with sweat, his lungs burning. He had pushed himself harder and harder, trying to drown out the storm inside him with the rhythmic pounding of his feet against the dry earth. But no matter how far he ran, Matteo's voice followed him.

"This is the only way. I have to protect you."

The memory hit him like a blow, and Noah stumbled, his knees buckling as he fell to the ground. He stayed there, hunched over, his hands pressed against the hot, cracked earth. His breath came in ragged gasps, and for a moment, he thought he might be sick.

Then the tears came.

They spilled out of him in ugly, choking sobs, his chest heaving as he pressed his face into his dusty hands. Every emotion he had been holding back—every ounce of anger, hurt, guilt, and love—rushed to the surface, breaking through the dam he had built around his heart. He cried until he couldn't breathe, until the world blurred around him and all he could feel was the ache in his chest.

For the first time, he let himself feel the fullness of what he had done. He let himself mourn the loss of Matteo—not just the boy he loved, but the version of himself that had existed with Matteo. The young man who had believed, even for a moment, that their love could survive in a world that seemed determined to tear them apart.

By the time Noah made it back to the house that evening, his eyes were swollen and his throat raw. He climbed the porch steps with heavy feet, each one echoing like a reminder of his guilt. Inside, the house was cool and quiet, the faint clink of dishes and low murmur of conversation coming from the dining room.

Noah stepped inside and made his way to the table, taking his usual seat.

Charles, sat at the table's head, his broad shoulders squared and his sharp blue eyes scanning the room like a hawk. Across from him, Garrett was already halfway through his meal, shovelling food into his mouth with the gracelessness of a teenage boy. Noah's mother, Mary, sat at the far end, her soft brown eyes darting nervously between her husband and her sons.

For a while, the only sounds were the scrape of forks against plates and the distant hum of the cicadas outside. Noah pushed his food around his plate, his appetite long gone, but he could feel his father's gaze on him, heavy and expectant.

"It's been quieter around here, hasn't it?" Garrett said suddenly, his smirk widening as he glanced at Noah. "Bet the bunkhouse smells better now, too."

Mary's sharp intake of breath cut through the silence, and she shot Garrett a warning look. "That's enough, Garrett," she said, her voice trembling slightly. She almost never raised her voice.

Garrett shrugged, unrepentant. "What? I'm just saying. It's not like they belonged here anyway."

Noah's hand tightened around his fork, his knuckles white. He could feel the anger rising in his chest, hot and suffocating, but he forced himself to take a steadying breath. The pain of the past week had been building inside him, and now it threatened to spill over again.

"I need to tell you something," Noah said suddenly, his voice cutting through the air like a blade. The clink of silverware against plates ceased immediately, the air in the room growing thick and heavy. All eyes turned to him, but he kept his gaze fixed on his plate. His heart pounded in his chest, his palms slick with sweat, but he forced the words out, each one like dragging glass from his throat. "Me and Matteo... we were together. For two years."

The silence that followed was deafening.

Garrett was the first to break it, his laugh sharp and mocking. "You're kidding, right?" he said, leaning back in his chair with a grin that didn't reach his eyes. "You and—what? You're gay now?"

"Garrett!" Mary snapped, her voice louder than Noah had ever heard it. She sat up straighter, her face pale, her lips trembling as she turned to her youngest son. "That is enough."

But Garrett shrugged, his smirk widening as he gestured toward Noah with his fork. "I mean, it makes sense, doesn't it? All that time he spent out in the fields with Matteo. Guess he wasn't just checking fences."

"Garrett!" Mary's voice cracked, her hands gripping the table as if she needed to steady herself. Her tone carried both anger and heartbreak, the weight of a mother who wanted to protect both of her sons from the world—and from each other.

But Garrett's voice was nothing compared to the scrape of Charles's chair against the hardwood floor as he stood. The sound cut through the room like a thunderclap, and the tension that had been simmering boiled over in an instant.

Charles towered over the table, his hands planted firmly on the surface as he leaned forward, his piercing blue eyes locking onto Noah like he was looking at a predator. "Tell me you're lying," he said, his voice low and dangerous, trembling not with fear but with rage barely contained. "Tell me you're not sitting at my table, in my house, saying this to my face."

Noah's throat tightened, his breath hitching as he forced himself to meet his father's gaze. "I'm not lying," he said, his voice steady despite the tears threatening to spill. "I loved him. I still love him."

Charles's lips curled into a sneer, his hands curling into fists. "Love," he spat, the word dripping with disdain. "You think that's what this is? You think throwing away everything this family has built, everything we stand for, is love? This is a house of God!" He bellowed.

"I haven't thrown anything away," Noah said, his voice breaking. "I'm still your son."

"No," Charles said, straightening and shaking his head. "You stopped being my son the moment you chose him over this family. Over everything I've worked my whole damn life to protect. Over God Himself." With Charles, that is what is always came back to – his version of the Lord – one whose love and protection extended only to those who looked and believed like Charles himself.

Mary gasped softly, her hand flying to her mouth, but Charles pressed on, his words relentless. "Do you have any idea what you've done? What you've risked? You've put this family in danger, Noah. You've put our reputation— our name—on the line for a damn farmhand."

Noah flinched at the venom in his father's voice, but he stood his ground, his chest heaving. "He's not just a farmhand," he said, his voice shaking with emotion. "He's—he's everything to me."

"And what do you think you are to him?" Charles shot back, his voice rising. "You think he loves you? You think he wouldn't sell you out in a heartbeat?"

"That's not true!" Noah shouted, his voice cracking as tears streamed down his face. "You don't know him! You don't know anything about us!"

Charles slammed his hand down on the table, the sound echoing through the room. "I know enough," he growled. "I know you've disgraced this family. I know you've put our reputation at risk for something that was never real. Something that goes against God!"

Noah's shoulders shook, his fists clenching at his sides. "It was real," he said through gritted teeth. "It is real."

Charles laughed, but there was no humour in it—only bitterness. "Not anymore," he said coldly. "You made sure of that when you brought this shame into my house."

"Shame?" Mary's voice trembled as she spoke, tears brimming in her eyes. "He's our son, Charles."

"Not anymore," Charles said, his gaze never leaving Noah. "Not until he remembers where he belongs, which is with a woman." He pointed toward the staircase, his hand shaking with barely contained rage. "Go upstairs. Pack your things. You're leaving this house tonight."

Noah stared at his father, his chest heaving, his vision blurred with tears. "You're kicking me out?" he asked, his voice trembling. "Because of this?"

"Because you've made your choice," Charles said, his voice cold as steel. "And it's not this family."

The words cut through Noah, and for a moment, he couldn't move, couldn't breathe. His hands fell limply to his sides, and he turned away, his chair scraping loudly against the floor as he stood. He walked toward the stairs with heavy, deliberate steps, his head bowed, his tears falling freely now.

Mary called after him, her voice trembling with desperation. "Noah—"

"Let him go," Charles said sharply, his tone final. "He made his bed. Now he can lie in it."

Even Garrett looked surprised at Charles' words. He kept his head down, eating the remainder of his dinner more slowly now.

Noah didn't stop, didn't look back. But the weight of his father's words settled over him like a crushing force, each step up the stairs feeling like a descent into something darker, something he wasn't sure he could climb out of.

Noah's room was dim, the only light coming from the lamp on his nightstand. A suitcase he'd hauled from the attic lay open on the bed, half-packed with clothes and belongings. He moved mechanically, his hands trembling as he folded a shirt and placed it in the bag. His mind was racing, his chest aching, but he forced himself to keep moving. He didn't know where he would go or what he would do, but he couldn't stay here—not after tonight. His father had made it clear that was not an option for him anyway.

The door creaked open behind him, and Noah turned to see his mother standing in the doorway. Her face was pale, her eyes red-rimmed, but there was determination in her expression that made Noah's chest tighten.

Mary stepped into the room, closing the door softly behind her. She crossed the room and sat down on the edge of the bed, her hands clasped tightly in her lap. For a long moment, neither of them spoke.

"I've known for a while," Mary said finally, her voice quiet. "I didn't want to say anything. I thought... maybe you'd tell me when you were ready. But I want you to know, Noah, I don't care who you love. I just care that you're happy."

Noah froze, his throat tightening as he blinked back tears. "You knew?" he asked, his voice barely more than a whisper.

Mary nodded, her eyes soft and full of understanding. "I saw the way you looked at him. The way he looked at you. I just... I hoped you'd be able to tell me someday. When you were ready."

Noah's tears spilled over then, and he turned away, pressing the back of his hand against his mouth to stifle a sob. Mary reached out, placing a gentle hand on his arm.

"I found a lawyer," she said, her voice trembling slightly. "She's in Eagle Pass. She helps families like Matteo's. I want to take you to see her tomorrow."

Noah stared at her, his chest heaving with emotion. For the first time in days, the tightness in his chest loosened, just a little. He nodded, his voice breaking as he whispered, "Thank you."

Mary smiled softly, her own tears spilling over as she reached for his hand. "You're my son, Noah. I'll always fight for you."

Noah sat motionless on the bed, his suitcase open beside him, half-filled with clothes he had thrown in without thought. The room was quiet, save for the distant hum of cicadas outside the window. The air inside felt thick, suffocating, like the walls had closed in around him. His father's voice still rang in his ears, cold and final, the weight of rejection pressing down on him like an anvil.

Across from him, Mary sat on the edge of the mattress, her hands clasped in her lap. She had always been a soft presence in the house, the quiet calm against Charles' fury. But tonight, there was something different in the way she held herself—an edge of steel beneath the sorrow in her eyes.

"I've already talked to the lawyer," she said, her voice gentle and full of hope. "Her name is Cara Donovan. She thinks there's a case to be made for Matteo and his family."

Noah's head snapped up, his heart hammering. "What?"

Mary nodded. "It's not going to be easy, but we can fight this. Matteo's family has been here for a long time. They have deep ties to the community, a history of steady employment, no criminal record. Those things work in their favour. If we can prove that deporting them would cause undue hardship, that they deserve to stay—"

Noah swallowed hard, his throat thick with emotion. "How?" His voice came out hoarse, desperate. "How do we fight this? They're already gone,

Mom. They're sitting in some ICE detention centre right now because of me."

Mary's expression didn't waver. "Because of a lot of things," she corrected. "Because of this country and the way it treats people like them. But we are not giving up."

Noah's chest ached, a sharp, splintering pain. "And Dad?" He scoffed, shaking his head. "You think he's going to let you spend money on a lawyer for them?"

Mary exhaled slowly, her hands tightening in her lap. "The ranch isn't his, Noah. It's mine. My family's."

Noah blinked, thrown by the words.

Mary gave him a small, knowing smile. "He likes to pretend otherwise, but the deed is in my name. My grandfather left it to me, not him." She hesitated for a moment, then reached out and took Noah's hand. "Besides, I have money set aside. Money he doesn't know about. Enough to help."

Noah stared at her, his throat closing up. He had spent his entire life thinking of his mother as quiet, passive—a woman who bent beneath the weight of Charles's will. But sitting here now, he saw her for what she truly was: a survivor.

"You need to leave tonight," Mary continued, squeezing his hand. "Your father's not going to let you stay. And if he finds out I'm helping, he'll make all of this harder for us."

Noah swallowed the lump in his throat. "Where am I supposed to go?"

Mary reached into her pocket and pulled out a small stack of bills, pressing them into his palm. "I booked you a room at a motel just outside of Eagle Pass. Tomorrow morning, we drive to Eagle Pass and meet the lawyer. She wants to talk to you, get your statement, start building the case."

Noah looked down at the money in his hand, his fingers trembling. He had been drowning for so long, lost in the weight of what he had done, in the unbearable guilt of Matteo's absence. But now, for the first time, he saw a way forward.

It wasn't enough to erase what he had done. It wouldn't bring Matteo back to him, wouldn't undo the betrayal. But maybe—just maybe—it could mean something.

Noah lifted his head, his vision blurred with unshed tears. "Thank you," he whispered.

Mary smiled, her own eyes shining. "You're my son," she said, her voice full of quiet, unwavering love. "I will always fight for you," she said again.

What If I Could Still Have Us?

The drive from the motel to Eagle Pass felt longer than it was. The road stretched endlessly ahead of them, the heat shimmering off the asphalt in hazy waves. Noah sat in the passenger seat of his mother's truck, his fingers drumming absently against his knee. He had barely slept the night before. The immensity of everything—the past, the guilt, the uncertainty—settled into his bones like an ache that wouldn't fade. Hi anxiousness continued as he faced the day ahead, the first day where his family truly knew him and who he was, with trepidation.

Mary drove with determination, her hands steady on the wheel, her lips pressed into a firm line. She had barely spoken since they left the motel that morning, but Noah knew her well enough to understand that she wasn't angry. She was focused. Her acceptance of him and her understanding of his pull to Matteo, a relief.

They pulled into the parking lot of a small law office tucked between a laundromat and a rundown diner. The sign above the door read: Donovan & Associates: Immigration Law.

Noah swallowed hard. This was it. The first step toward making things right.

Inside, the office was small but tidy, the walls lined with bookshelves filled with thick legal volumes. A woman sat behind a desk, flipping through a file. She looked up when they entered and offered a polite smile.

"You must be the Calloways," she said, standing. "I'm Cara Donovan."

Noah recognized her name immediately, but the woman in front of him wasn't what he had expected. She was young—maybe in her early thirties

—with dark brown hair pulled into a loose bun and intelligent green eyes framed by black-rimmed glasses. She carried herself with confidence, her gaze sharp, assessing.

Noah cleared his throat, shifting awkwardly. "Yeah. I'm Noah. This is my mom, Mary."

Cara nodded, gesturing toward the chairs in front of her desk. "Come sit down. Let's talk."

They sat, and Cara settled into the chair across from them, flipping open a notepad. "I appreciate you reaching out," she said. "I know this isn't an easy situation."

Noah's jaw tightened. That was an understatement.

"I read through the preliminary details your mother sent me," Cara continued, her tone calm but focused. "Matteo and his family were taken in an ICE raid a week ago. They've lived and worked on your ranch for more than 15 years, and they have no criminal record. Is that correct?"

Noah nodded stiffly. "Yeah. None of them do. They are good people." He wished he had kept that in mind before reporting them.

Cara glanced at Mary. "And you own the ranch?"

Mary hesitated for only a second before nodding. "Technically, yes. It was my grandfather's land before mine. Charles—my husband—runs it, but the deed is in my name."

Cara leaned back slightly, considering. "That gives us an angle. Matteo's family has been gainfully employed for more than a decade under your ownership. We can argue that deportation would cause undue hardship not only to them, but to the business itself."

Noah sat forward, his pulse quickening. "So we can fight this?"

Cara met his gaze directly. "Yes. But it won't be easy."

The hope that had sparked in his chest dimmed slightly. "What are their chances?"

Cara sighed, folding her hands on the desk. "Immigration law is tough. Even with strong community ties and no criminal record, ICE is aggressive with deportations, especially under the Langford administration. But there are options. We can file a request for a 'Cancellation of Removal' on the grounds that Matteo's family has been here long enough to establish significant roots. They've worked, paid taxes, contributed to the economy. If we can prove they would suffer extreme hardship if deported, they may be eligible for relief."

Noah's hands clenched into fists. "How long would that take?"

Cara's expression softened. "Months. Maybe longer, especially with all of the cases going through the courts now."

Noah exhaled sharply, dragging a hand through his hair. He had hoped—naively, maybe—that this would be simpler. That they could just fix it. Noah had envisioned Matteo returning that very night, but this time with the freedom to be who they truly were. But nothing was that easy.

Mary reached out, placing a steadying hand on his knee. "We'll fight," she said firmly. "We'll do whatever it takes."

Cara nodded. "I'll also file a request for parole. It's a long shot, but if we can argue that Matteo and his family aren't flight risks, ICE might release them while we fight the case. If they stay detained, this becomes much harder."

Noah swallowed. "So what do we need to do?"

Cara reached for a legal pad and clicked her pen. "We start gathering evidence. We need letters of support from people who know Matteo and his family—neighbours, coworkers, anyone willing to testify to their character and contributions. I'll also need employment records, pay stubs, and any documentation proving their long-term presence here."

Mary nodded. "I can get that."

Cara turned to Noah. "And you."

Noah stiffened. "Me?"

"I need your statement," she said simply. "You've known Matteo for years. You can testify to his character. If you're willing to go on record about your relationship, it could be powerful."

Noah's breath caught. He felt Mary's eyes on him, but he couldn't look at her. He had only just told his family. He feared what a more public proclamation might mean, and how people would look at him if they knew.

Cara didn't push. "Think about it," she said. "It's not an easy decision, and I won't force you into it. But the more personal this case is, the harder it will be for ICE to argue that Matteo is just another name on a list."

Noah swallowed hard, nodding. He wasn't sure he was ready for that. But he had already betrayed Matteo once. If this was his chance to undo some of the damage, how could he refuse?

Cara slid a card across the desk. "I'll file the necessary paperwork today. In the meantime, start gathering everything you can. The sooner we move, the better."

Noah took the card, his fingers curling around it.

Cara gave him a long look. "I know this feels impossible right now. But I've fought cases like this before. And sometimes, we win."

For the first time in days, something shifted inside Noah. It wasn't relief—not yet—but it was something. A flicker of hope, fragile but real.

He met Cara's gaze and nodded. "Then let's win."

The evening heat sat heavy over the ranch, the last of the day's light painting the sky in bands of orange and violet. Noah sat in the truck beside his mother, staring straight ahead as she pulled onto the long, winding gravel road that led up to their house. His hands were curled into fists in his lap, his breath slow and steady, but his mind was anything but calm.

The meeting with Cara had lit something inside him—something that had been flickering ever since the raid, ever since he watched Matteo disappear into the back of that van. But now, it was a steady flame. He had made his choice.

He was going to fight.

But there was still a battle waiting for him at home.

As Mary parked the truck in front of the house, Noah exhaled sharply, trying to steel himself. The porch light cast long shadows across the worn wooden steps. Inside, he knew his father was waiting, just as he knew that nothing he said tonight would change Charles Calloway's mind.

But Noah wasn't walking away this time.

Charles was sitting at the dining table when they walked in, the dim light from the overhead lamp casting deep shadows across his face. His Bible lay open in front of him, the pages worn and marked with ink from years of notes in the margins. He didn't look up right away. He simply flipped a page, ran a slow hand over his chin, and sighed.

"I know where you've both been," he said finally, his voice low, rough. "You think you can fight to bring that boy back here."

Noah swallowed hard. "Then you know what I'm about to say."

Charles closed the Bible and folded his hands over it, finally lifting his gaze. His eyes, the same piercing blue as Noah's, were cold. "I know you think this is what you have to do," he said, his voice measured, careful. "But I need you to hear me now, son. You are walking down a road that leads nowhere good."

Noah took a step forward, his fists still clenched at his sides. "You let them work this land for nearly fifteen years," he said, his voice shaking with frustration. "You knew. You knew they weren't legal, and you still gave them work. Because it was the Christian thing to do."

Charles nodded, his expression unreadable. "Because it was," he said simply. "A man has a right to provide for his family. I knew what they were, but I also knew they were honest, hardworking people. I let them work because it was right. You're the one who had them sent away. I have to believe that you did that because a part of you knew what you and that boy were doing was nothing but shameful." Charles wasn't yelling yet, but the edge of disgust in his voice was apparent.

Noah's breath hitched, and for a moment, he felt like a child again, standing in the same kitchen, arguing with a father who never bent. "So, you won't help us?" he asked, his voice cracking. "You won't help us keep them here?"

Charles shook his head. "I can't."

The words struck like a slap.

"I have already done what I could for them, Noah," Charles said, his voice steady and firm. "But I will not go against the will of God to fight for this."

Noah's heart clenched, his stomach twisting violently. He knew what was coming, but hearing it still burned.

Charles leaned forward, his hands pressing against the Bible as if grounding himself in his faith. "You are my son," he said, his voice thick with something that sounded like grief. "And I love you, Noah. But I cannot support this. I cannot stand behind you in this fight. Because I believe in God."

Noah let out a bitter laugh, shaking his head. "And God says I don't deserve love?"

Charles exhaled through his nose, his fingers gripping the edges of his Bible. "God says a great many things. But He is clear on this. What you and that boy were doing is a sin."

Noah's chest tightened. "You think I chose this?" His voice rose, the heat inside him flaring as he took another step forward. "You think I wanted to love someone in a way that makes you hate me?"

"I do not hate you," Charles said firmly, standing now, his shoulders squared. "But I hate the sin. And what you are doing, what you are fighting for—it is sin."

Noah shook his head, stepping back as if putting space between them might make the words sting less. "You think I'm bringing shame to this family," he said, his voice quieter now.

The kitchen was silent, the air heavy with words spoken and unspoken. Charles's gaze didn't waver, his piercing blue eyes fixed on Noah like a judge delivering a final verdict. "I think you already have," he said, his voice cold and resolute.

Noah felt something inside him crack. A part of him had always held on to the smallest sliver of hope that his father would bend, just a little. That somewhere, beneath the weight of his beliefs, there was love for Noah that would outweigh his need to be right and righteous.

But there wasn't.

Noah nodded slowly, pressing his lips together, forcing down the lump in his throat. "I guess that's that, then," he said, turning toward the stairs. His footsteps were heavy against the hardwood, each step echoing in the hollow silence of the room.

"Noah," Charles called after him, his voice softer now, almost hesitant.

Noah paused but didn't turn around. He was done begging for something that was never going to come.

But before he could take another step, Mary stood from her chair, her hands trembling as she gripped the back of it. "Enough," she said quietly, her voice shaking.

Both Charles and Noah turned to look at her. Mary rarely spoke with such authority, but there was a fire in her eyes now, a determination that made Noah's chest tighten.

"Charles," she said, her voice steadying as she stepped forward. "I have loved you for over twenty years. I have followed you, supported you, believed in you. But I will not stand here and watch you reject our son."

Charles's jaw tightened, his gaze darkening. "Mary, this isn't about—"

"It's about love," she interrupted, her voice rising. "The kind of love that isn't conditional. The kind of love that doesn't stop because of what a preacher or a book says." She squared her shoulders, her chin lifting. "This ranch—this house—it's mine. My grandfather left it to me, not you. And if you don't want to be under the same roof as our son, then you can leave."

Charles froze, his expression unreadable. For a long moment, the only sound was the faint hum of cicadas outside the window. Then he straightened, his lips pressing into a thin line. Without another word, he turned and walked out of the kitchen, his boots thudding against the floor as he disappeared into the hall. The screen door slammed shut before the blast of Charles' truck starting up filled the room.

Noah stared at his mother, his chest tight, his throat burning. "Mom," he started, his voice breaking.

Mary turned to him, her eyes softening as she reached for his hand. "I'm not losing you, Noah," she said simply. "Not for anything. Not for anyone."

*****

The next morning, the air in Cara Donovan's office was cool and still, the faint scent of coffee lingering in the space. Noah sat at the small desk across from Cara, a sheet of paper in front of him. His hands trembled slightly as he picked up the pen, the weight of what he was about to write pressing down on him like the Texas sun.

"This statement will be submitted as part of the parole request for Matteo and his family," Cara explained gently. "It needs to show the depth of his ties to this country, to you, to the community. But more than that, it needs to show the humanity behind the names on the deportation list."

Noah nodded, his throat tight. He glanced at his mother, who sat quietly in the corner, her presence steady and supportive. Then he looked back at the blank page in front of him and began to write.

Matteo and I met when we were kids. His family worked on my family's ranch, and from the very beginning, there was something about him that drew me in. Matteo has always been kind, steady, and hardworking in a way that I admired but didn't understand until we were older.

We became friends before we even knew what that word meant. We would race horses across the fields, climb the old oak tree behind the barn, and talk for hours about everything and nothing. He taught me Spanish, and I taught him how to fish, though he was always better at it than I was.

When we were seventeen, our friendship became something more. I don't know how to explain it except to say that loving Matteo felt as natural as breathing. It wasn't something I chose. It was just... us.

But we had to hide it. His family wouldn't have understood. Mine wouldn't have accepted it. So we built our love in secret places—on the hill overlooking the ranch, in the old barn, in moments that were never enough but always everything.

Matteo is not just a worker or an "illegal immigrant." He is the hardest-working person I've ever known. He's a son, a brother, a part of this community in ways that most people will never see because they don't look closely enough. He is good and kind and brave, and he deserves better than what this country is doing to him and his family.

When ICE came, I stood on the porch and watched them take him away. I will never forgive myself for that. But I am here now, writing this, because I want to make it right. I want Matteo to come home. I want him to know that he is loved, that he belongs, that he matters.

I am not proud of what I did. But I am proud of him. And I will do whatever it takes to bring him back.

I am asking for your help in bringing Matteo and his family back to the community that needs them, to the land they've worked, and to the *people who love them. Matteo doesn't deserve to be punished for seeking a better life, for building something here, or for loving someone who could never stop loving him in return.*

This is not just about justice. This is about humanity. About doing what's right.

Please, let him come home,
Noah Calloway

Noah set the pen down, his chest heaving as he exhaled shakily. He felt raw, exposed, like he had poured every piece of himself onto the page. He looked up at Cara, who read the statement silently, her sharp green eyes scanning each word.

When she finished, she looked at him, her expression softening. "This is strong," she said. "It's personal. It's powerful. It's exactly what we need."

Noah nodded, his throat too tight to speak.

Cara gave him a small, encouraging smile. "I'll file this with the parole request today. With any luck, we'll hear something soon."

*****

It was two weeks later when Cara called. Noah was sitting on the porch, his boots resting on the railing, the sun dipping low in the sky. The phone buzzed in his pocket, and he answered it with shaking hands.

"They're being released," Cara said, her voice bright with restrained excitement. "The parole request was approved."

Noah's breath hitched, his chest tightening. "They're... they're coming home?"

"They'll still have to go through the legal process," Cara cautioned. "But for now, yes. Matteo and his family will be released into community custody."

Noah leaned back in his chair, his eyes closing as relief washed over him like cool water. He felt the tears spill over, but for the first time in weeks, they weren't tears of guilt or grief. They were tears of hope.

Noah sat on the porch, the phone still in his hand, the faint hum of cicadas filling the space around him. His chest felt tight, like it might burst from the weight of everything he'd been holding in. They were being released. Matteo and his family were coming home.

The words echoed in his mind, over and over, like a mantra he was afraid to believe. He could still hear Cara's voice—calm and measured—tempering her excitement with caution: "They'll still have to go through the legal process, but for now, yes, they'll be released into community custody."

For now.

The words clung to him like a shadow, but he pushed them aside. It was enough for now. It was a chance, and he would take it.

Noah leaned back, letting his head fall against the wood of the chair. Above him, the stars blinked into existence one by one, their faint light piercing through the lingering twilight. He'd grown up under this same sky, on this same porch, but tonight it felt different. Lighter, maybe. Or maybe that was just him.

"Are you all right?" Mary's voice broke through the stillness, and he turned to see her standing in the doorway, her expression soft, concerned.

Noah nodded, his throat too tight to speak.

Mary stepped out onto the porch, crossing to him with slow, deliberate steps. She placed a hand on his shoulder, her grip gentle but steady. "You did good," she said softly.

Noah let out a shaky breath, his lips trembling as he fought to keep the tears at bay. "I don't know if it's enough," he admitted, his voice barely above a whisper.

Mary squeezed his shoulder. "It's a start. And sometimes, that's all we can ask for."

He nodded, staring out at the darkened fields stretching endlessly before them. Somewhere out there, Matteo was waiting.

"I'm going to sponsor them," Noah said suddenly, the words spilling out before he could stop them. He turned to his mother, his eyes wide, pleading. "When they get back, I need to see him. I need to tell him..."

Mary smiled gently, brushing a stray curl from his forehead. "You'll tell him," she said. "When the time is right, you'll tell him everything."

The knot in Noah's chest loosened, just a little, and he leaned into his mother's touch, letting her warmth steady him.

Down Bad

The evening sun cast long shadows over the Calloway ranch as a dust trail curled up from the gravel road, marking the arrival of a vehicle. The light had softened into that deep Texan gold, painting the fields in amber hues, but the heat of the day still clung to the air, thick and dry. Noah stood on the porch, hands braced against the railing, his stomach tight with nerves.

He had waited for this moment for weeks.

The black SUV rolled to a stop near the small cottage Matteo and his family had lived in, the government plates catching the last sliver of sunlight before the door opened. Matteo's mother stepped out first, her dark hair pinned back, her shoulders squared with a kind of prideful resilience. Then his father, Héctor, his face lined with exhaustion, but his posture unbent, the weight of survival carried on his back as it always had been. Matteo's sister came next.

Then Matteo.

Noah's breath caught.

Matteo stepped out of the vehicle like a man returning to a battlefield, his movements careful, deliberate. He had lost weight, the sharp angles of his face more pronounced, the darkness under his eyes deeper. But his presence—his force—hadn't dimmed. He stood tall, his gaze scanning the ranch he had known his whole life, his jaw tight.

Noah wanted to move, wanted to say something, anything, but his feet stayed planted.

Matteo's eyes found him.

A moment stretched between them, thick as the Texas heat.

Noah saw the flicker of something there—recognition, resentment, something unspoken that Noah couldn't put his finger on. Then Matteo looked away.

Mary came down the porch steps, smoothing her hands over her dress as she approached Matteo's mother. She spoke in low, reassuring tones, touching the woman's shoulder, guiding them toward the house they had lived in for so many years. The rest of the ranch hands gathered outside the nearby bunkhouse, watching the scene unfold with wary eyes, murmured words passing between them.

Matteo said nothing as he helped his mother and sister gather their belongings, leading them toward the small house they had once been forced to leave behind. He didn't look at Noah again.

Noah exhaled slowly, a tightness settling into his chest. He turned, stepping off the porch, his boots crunching against the dry earth as he followed at a distance.

Héctor lingered by the truck, speaking with one of the agents, his voice too low for Noah to make out. Matteo was just ahead, a duffel slung over his shoulder as he stepped inside the house, the door left ajar. Noah hesitated for only a moment before following. The house smelled the same—warm spices, the faint scent of woodsmoke that had seeped into its bones over the years. Matteo dropped his bag by the kitchen table, bracing his hands against the surface, his back to Noah.

Noah swallowed hard. "Matteo—"

"Don't." Matteo's voice was sharp, his shoulders tense.

Noah flinched but didn't back away. "I just—"

"You think you can just say something and it'll make this better?" Matteo turned then, his eyes dark, unreadable. "You think words are enough for what you did?"

Noah felt his stomach drop. "I was trying to fix it."

Matteo let out a short, humourless laugh. "Fix it?" His voice was quiet, controlled, but the anger beneath it crackled like dry wood catching flame. "You called them. You let them take us."

Noah's throat tightened. "I thought—well, I didn't think. I was angry," Noah confessed.

Matteo's expression twisted, something breaking in his gaze. "Yeah, Noah. You were angry, so you blew up my life, attacked not just me, but my family." His voice dropped lower. "You didn't care what it cost me."

Noah's breath caught. "That's not true."

Matteo scoffed, shaking his head. "Then tell me, when they put those cuffs on me, when they threw my family in the back of those vans—where were you? Watching from your goddamn porch?" He took a step closer, his voice sharp. "Did you feel powerful, Noah? Did it make you feel safe?"

Noah shook his head, his voice raw. "I hated myself for it."

Matteo exhaled, his chest rising and falling with the weight of it. "You don't get to hate yourself," he said, his voice quieter now, but no less sharp. "Not after what you did."

Noah reached for him then, desperation clawing at his ribs. "Matteo, please—"

Matteo stepped back. "Don't."

The space between them felt impossible.

"I agreed with my family we had to leave because I didn't want anything to happen to you," Matteo continued, his voice bitter. "Because despite everything, I loved you. And you—you handed us over."

Noah's vision blurred, the weight of it all pressing down on him. "I will never forgive myself for it."

Matteo's lips parted slightly, a flicker of something passing through his expression. Then he shook his head, his jaw setting. "Good." He stepped past Noah, his shoulder brushing against his as he moved toward the hallway. He paused in the doorway, his back still to him.

"This is over, Noah," Matteo said, his voice steady. "Whatever we were... it's done."

Noah felt the finality of it like a knife to the gut. He wanted to fight, to say something that could fix this, but there was nothing. He had set fire to what they were, and now he had to watch it burn.

Matteo disappeared into the hallway, and the soft click of a door closing behind him echoed through the quiet little house.

Noah stood there, staring at the empty space where Matteo had been. His hands trembled at his sides, his breath unsteady.

Outside, the cicadas droned on, indifferent to the ache settling deep in Noah's chest. The sun had nearly set, casting the last of its golden light over the ranch, turning everything to shadow.

Noah turned and walked out the door.

This time, he didn't look back.

You've Reached The End But...
The Stories Never Stop

Songs To Stories is exactly what it sounds like—short, emotionally devastating, romantically charged, and occasionally unhinged novellas inspired by the one and only Taylor Swift. Because why simply listen to a song when you can spiral into an entire fictional universe about it?

A new novella drops on the 13th of every month, so if you have commitment issues, don't worry—you don't have to wait long for your next dose of heartbreak, longing, and characters making wildly questionable life choices in the name of love.

To keep up with the latest releases, visit BrittWolfe.com—or don't, and risk missing out while the rest of us are already crying over the next one. Your call.

See you at the next emotional wreckage.

About The Author
Britt Wolfe

Britt Wolfe was born in Fort McMurray, Alberta, and now lives in Calgary, where she battles snow, writes stories, and cries over Taylor Swift lyrics like the proud elder Swiftie she is. She loves being part of a fan base that's as passionate as it is melodramatic.

She's married to a smoking hot Australian (her words, but also probably everyone else's), and together they parent two fur-babies: Sophie, the most perfect husky in the universe, and Lena, a mischievous cat who keeps them on their toes—and their furniture in shreds.

When Britt's not writing or re-listening to "All Too Well (10 Minute Version)," she's indulging her love for reading, potatoes in all forms, and the colour green. She's also a huge fan of polar bears, tigers, red pandas, otters, Nile crocodiles, and—because they're underrated—donkeys.

Her life is full of love, laughter, and just enough chaos to keep things interesting.

 @the.banality.of.britt

 BrittWolfe.com

www.ingramcontent.com/pod-product-compliance
Lightning Source LLC
Chambersburg PA
CBHW082250120626
46555CB00009B/3027